W9-DEZ-666

GO WEST!
Travel to the Wild Frontier

GO WEST WITH
FAMOUS TRAILBLAZERS

Rachel Stuckey

Crabtree Publishing Company
www.crabtreebooks.com

Crabtree Publishing Company
www.crabtreebooks.com

Author: Rachel Stuckey

Consultant: Professor Patricia Loughlin, University of Central Oklahoma

Managing Editor: Tim Cooke

Designer: Lynne Lennon

Picture Manager: Sophie Mortimer

Design Manager: Keith Davis

Editorial Director: Lindsey Lowe

Project Coordinator: Kathy Middleton

Proofreaders: Wendy Scavuzzo and Petrice Custance

Editor: Janine Deschenes

Children's Publisher: Anne O'Daly

Production coordinator and Prepress techician: Tammy McGarr

Print coordinator: Katherine Bertie

Production coordinated by Brown Bear Books

Photographs:
Front Cover: **Alamy:** Glasshouse Images bt; **Corbis:** Bettmann main; **Library of Congress** tr.

Interior: **Bridgeman Images:** 13tl; **Kemper Art Museum:** 6tl; **Library of Congress:** 6, 6br, 11tr, 11br, 12, 16, 17tr, 19bl, 20tl, 21, 24, 25br, 28; **Rochkind:** 19tr; **Shutterstock:** Kobby Dagani 29br, Ensuper 15b, Everett Historical 14, 15tr, 22, 23tl, 23br, 26br, 27tr, 27br, f11photo 29tl, Welcomia 4bl; **Thinkstock:** Capturelight 18, Jeremy Edwards 4tr, Hidesy 26c, MarkUK97 25tl; **Topfoto:** The Granger Collection 7, 10, 13br, 17bl, 20br, 25bl.; **Public Domain:** 24rc

All other artwork and maps **Brown Bear Books Ltd.**

Brown Bear Books has made every attempt to contact the copyright holder. If you have any information please contact licensing@brownbearbooks.co.uk

Library and Archives Canada Cataloguing in Publication

Stuckey, Rachel, author
      Go West with famous trailblazers / Rachel Stuckey.

(Go West! travel to the wild frontier)
Includes index.
Issued in print and electronic formats.
ISBN 978-0-7787-2324-0 (bound).--
ISBN 978-0-7787-2337-0 (paperback).--
ISBN 978-1-4271-1733-5 (html)

      1. Explorers--Juvenile literature. 2. West (U.S.)--Discovery and exploration--Juvenile literature. 3. Frontier and pioneer life--Juvenile literature. I. Title.

F592.S83 2016   j978   C2015-907968-3
                                                      C2015-907969-1

Library of Congress Cataloging-in-Publication Data

Names: Stuckey, Rachel, author.
Title: Go west with famous trailblazers / Rachel Stuckey.
Description: New York, New York : Crabtree Publishing Company, 2016. | Series: Go west! Travel to the wild frontier | Includes index. | Description based on print version record and CIP data provided by publisher; resource not viewed.
Identifiers: LCCN 2015051399 (print) | LCCN 2015049841 (ebook) | ISBN 9781427117335 (electronic HTML) | ISBN 9780778723240 (reinforced library binding : alk. paper) | ISBN 9780778723370 (pbk. : alk. paper)
Subjects: LCSH: West (U.S.)--Discovery and exploration--Juvenile literature. | Explorers--West (U.S.)--History--Juvenile literature. | Pioneers--West (U.S.)--History--Juvenile literature. | West (U.S.)--History--Juvenile literature. | Frontier and pioneer life--West (U.S.)--Juvenile literature.
Classification: LCC F592 (print) | LCC F592 .S845 2016 (ebook) | DDC 978/.02--dc23
LC record available at http://lccn.loc.gov/2015051399

Crabtree Publishing Company

www.crabtreebooks.com   1-800-387-7650

Printed in Canada/022016/IH20151223

Published in Canada
Crabtree Publishing
616 Welland Ave.
St. Catharines, Ontario
L2M 5V6

Published in the United States
Crabtree Publishing
PMB 59051
350 Fifth Avenue, 59th Floor
New York, New York 10118

Published in the United Kingdom
Crabtree Publishing
Maritime House
Basin Road North, Hove
BN41 1WR

Published in Australia
Crabtree Publishing
3 Charles Street
Coburg North
VIC, 3058

CONTENTS

Opening the West

In 1800, Spain, Great Britain, and France claimed land west of the Mississippi River in North America. Within decades, the whole region would belong to the United States.

ALREADY HERE

★ "Empty" land not empty

★ Inhabited for many centuries

In 1800, the West was already inhabited by hundreds of groups of Native peoples. On the plains lived the Lakota (Sioux) and Cheyenne, as well as the Ojibwa, Blackfoot, and Cree First Nations in Canada. The Southwest was home to the Apache, Navajo, and others. Pacific Coast peoples included the Chinook, while the Nez Percé and other nations lived in the foothills of the Rocky Mountains.

Above: The cliff houses of Mesa Verde in Colorado were built by the Pueblo peoples before 1300.

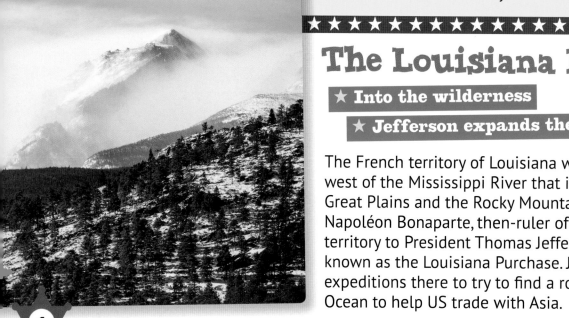

The Louisiana Purchase

★ Into the wilderness

★ Jefferson expands the nation

The French territory of Louisiana was a vast region west of the Mississippi River that included the Great Plains and the Rocky Mountains. In 1803, Napoléon Bonaparte, then-ruler of France, sold the territory to President Thomas Jefferson in what was known as the Louisiana Purchase. Jefferson later sent expeditions there to try to find a route to the Pacific Ocean to help US trade with Asia.

War with Mexico

★ **California, Texas, Southwest all won**

In 1845, Texas joined the United States. However, President James K. Polk wanted even more territory in the Southwest. He claimed a border region of Mexico, invading in 1846 and declaring war on Mexico. The United States defeated the Mexican armies in 1847. In 1848, a peace **treaty** passed control of the Southwest and California to the US government.

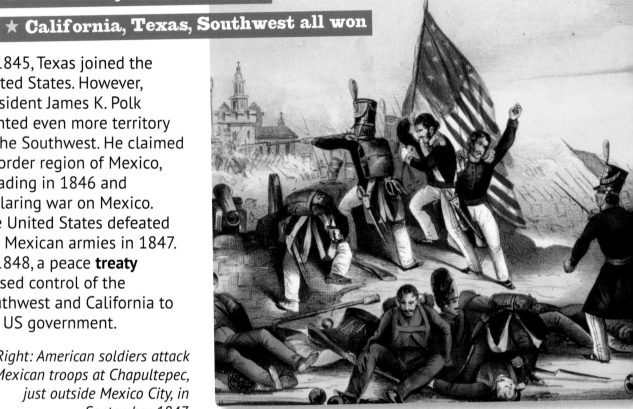

Right: American soldiers attack Mexican troops at Chapultepec, just outside Mexico City, in September 1847.

Manifest Destiny

★ **Dominance is inevitable**

★ **Resistance is pointless**

Many Americans believed it was their right to take ownership of land in the West. In 1845, a newspaper editor named John O'Sullivan called this idea the "**manifest destiny**" of America. Manifest means obvious or very clear. Although not everyone agreed, the idea became popular. It inspired President Polk's decision to buy Oregon from the British in 1846. It also led to the war with Mexico in the same year.

DID YOU KNOW?

Mexico won its independence from Spain in 1821. Mexico owned Texas, but it allowed Americans to settle there. In 1835, Texas colonists rebelled against the Mexican government. After a bloody war, they declared independence in 1836 as the Republic of Texas.

Exploring New Territory

The first American explorers of the new West traveled on foot, on horseback, and by canoe, as the Native peoples did. These **trailblazers** mapped the way for settlers to follow.

THE FIRST EXPANSION

★ **Across the Appalachians**

★ **Boone blazes a trail**

The Appalachian Mountains blocked the way for settlers to move west from the East Coast beyond Virginia. In 1775, the **mountain man** Daniel Boone had **blazed** a trail through the Cumberland Gap, a pass through the mountains. The track allowed later settlers to cross the mountains to the **frontier** areas of Kentucky and Tennessee.

Left: Daniel Boone leads settlers through the Cumberland Gap to Kentucky.

Lewis & Clark

★ **Traveling coast to coast**

★ **Two-year journey**

Right: Members of Lewis and Clark's expedition use guns to scare off grizzly bears.

In 1804, President Jefferson sent Meriwether Lewis and William Clark to explore the new Louisiana Territory. Jefferson hoped to find a route to the Pacific Ocean to enable trade with Asia. Lewis and Clark reached the Pacific two years after they left. They returned with information about the geography, **resources**, and peoples of the West.

NATIVE GUIDE

★ **Sacagawea shows the way**

★ **Helps keep the peace**

Lewis and Clark led a large team known as the Corps of Discovery. Its most famous member was a young Shoshone woman named Sacagawea. Captured by the Hidatsa as a young girl, Sacagawea later married a French-Canadian fur trader who lived among the Mandan on the Missouri River. Sacagawea acted as a guide and translator for Lewis and Clark. The presence of a young Native woman in the Corps helped convince Native nations that the expedition was not aggressive or warlike.

Right: Sacagawea helps Lewis and Clark plan their journey. She was familiar with trails and landmarks from her youth.

DID YOU KNOW?

Alexander Mackenzie crossed Canada in 1793 to become the first European to reach the Arctic and Pacific oceans in North America. He followed the canoe and land routes of the Dene and Nuxalk people, beating Lewis and Clark to the Pacific Ocean by ten years.

Zebulon Pike

★ **Explorer heads south**

★ **Captured by Spanish**

As Lewis and Clark explored northern Louisiana, President Jefferson sent Captain Zebulon Pike to explore the southern part. While in Colorado, Pike traveled into Mexican territory and was taken prisoner by the Spanish army. While Pike was a prisoner, he gathered information about Colorado. After Pike's release, he returned to the United States with information about Colorado. The information was used by settlers heading to Colorado after it became part of the United States in 1848.

Where in the West?

CANADA

UNITED STATES

Oregon Compromise
Under a treaty signed in 1818, the United States and Great Britain both occupied Oregon Territory. Joint occupation became strained after 1842, however, when the Oregon Trail from the East was extended and many American settlers arrived in Oregon. In 1846, the United States signed a treaty with Great Britain which set a border between Oregon and British territory in Canada.

Mexican Cession
California and much of the Southwest were handed from Mexico to the United States after the American victory in the Mexican–American War (1846–1848). The handover of land was part of the Treaty of Guadalupe Hidalgo.

Gadsden Purchase
In 1853, the US ambassador in Mexico, Joseph Gadsden, agreed to buy Mexican land. The United States wanted the land to build a southern transcontinental railroad to the Pacific Coast. The land is now part of Arizona and New Mexico.

Texas Annexation
In the early 19th century, many American settlers moved into the Mexican province of Texas. In 1835, these "Texians" declared independence. After a war with Mexico, the Republic of Texas was formed in 1836. In 1845, Texas became part of the United States.

As the United States grew larger through a series of land acquisitions in the 1800s, trailblazers explored the new territories in the West.

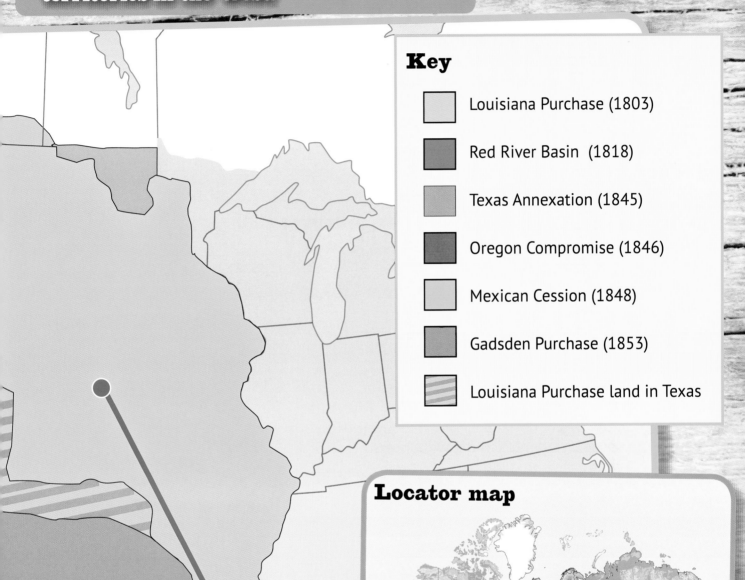

Key

- ☐ Louisiana Purchase (1803)
- ☐ Red River Basin (1818)
- ☐ Texas Annexation (1845)
- ☐ Oregon Compromise (1846)
- ☐ Mexican Cession (1848)
- ☐ Gadsden Purchase (1853)
- ☐ Louisiana Purchase land in Texas

Locator map

Louisiana Purchase

President Thomas Jefferson's purchase of Louisiana from the French in 1803 nearly doubled the size of the United States. The 828,000 square miles (2,144,510 sq km) of land covered all or part of what are now 15 US states and two Canadian provinces.

Trappers and Mountain Men

Many of the first Europeans to explore North America were fur trappers. They often lived among the Native people, marrying and starting families with Native women.

Hudson's Bay Company

★ **Traders in the wilderness**

★ **British control fur trade**

Founded by the English in 1670, the Hudson's Bay Company was the first fur-trading business. It controlled the vast territory north and west of the British colonies in North America for over 150 years. Many trailblazers were fur trappers. They delivered furs to the company's depots in the **wilderness.**

DID YOU KNOW?

After Canadian confederation in 1867, the Hudson's Bay Company remained a huge landowner. The company branched into retail sales in the later 1800s. Today, the company operates a chain of department stores.

The Fur Traders

★ **Americans join the trade**

★ **Mountain men in the Rockies**

In the 1800s, new companies competed with the Hudson's Bay Company. John Jacob Astor formed the American Fur Trading Company in 1808, which grew into a huge trade empire. William H. Ashley formed the Rocky Mountain Fur Company in 1823. His men discovered the South Pass through the Rockies, making it possible for wagon trains to cross the mountains. Ashley made a fortune and retired in 1827.

Right: A fur trapper waters his horses in a stream in the Rocky Mountains.

JAMES O. PATTIE

★ **Trapper writes his story**

★ **Captured by Mexico**

James O. Pattie was one of the few mountain men to write about his experiences. He grew up on the frontier in Missouri. He was a skilled hunter and woodsman, and joined a fur-trapping expedition to Arizona in 1824. Arizona was then Mexican territory, and Pattie was captured by the Mexican army. After returning to the United States, he published *The Personal Narrative of James O. Pattie* in 1831.

Frontier Scout

★ **Kit Carson in the West**

★ **Guides expeditions**

At age 16, Christopher "Kit" Carson (right) left home to become a fur trapper. In the 1830s, he joined expeditions into the Rockies and California. He lived among Native peoples and worked as an **interpreter**. In the 1840s, he joined John C. Frémont's expedition to map the West. Frémont's reports and sensational stories in **dime novels** made Carson famous.

THE LIFE OF OLD BILL

★ **Old Bill at home in the West**

★ **Learns Native languages**

William S. Williams, known as "Old Bill," was an expert trapper and interpreter. He first started learning Native American languages in the War of 1812, when he fought for the United States against the British. In the 1820s, he became an interpreter and guide on expeditions to the West. He married the daughter of an Osage chief and worked as a trapper, guide, and interpreter. In 1849, he was **ambushed** and killed by Ute warriors during a conflict between Native peoples.

Right: Williams explored large parts of Texas, California, Arizona, and Colorado.

TRAPPERS AND MOUNTAIN MEN

The Gold Rush

In the early 1840s, California was Mexican territory with a few small coastal settlements. Few European settlers traveled there. But all that changed in 1848, when gold was discovered and the territory became part of the United States.

An Early Californian

★ **Sutter builds a fort**

★ **Sitting on a goldmine**

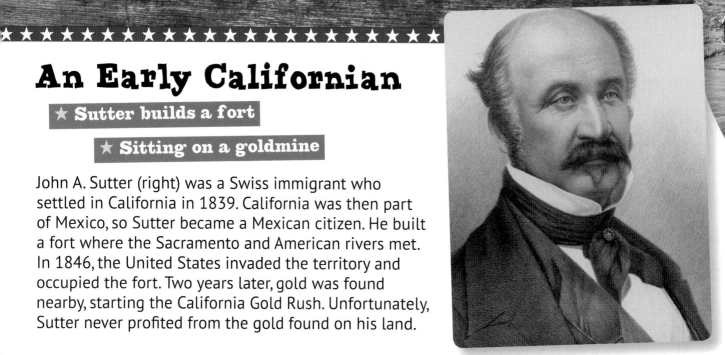

John A. Sutter (right) was a Swiss immigrant who settled in California in 1839. California was then part of Mexico, so Sutter became a Mexican citizen. He built a fort where the Sacramento and American rivers met. In 1846, the United States invaded the territory and occupied the fort. Two years later, gold was found nearby, starting the California Gold Rush. Unfortunately, Sutter never profited from the gold found on his land.

MY WESTERN JOURNAL

Imagine you heard about a gold rush. Do you think you would be tempted to give up everything to join in? Give your reasons for or against heading for the goldfields.

SPREADING THE NEWS

★ **Brannan whips up interest ...**

... and makes himself rich

In 1845, a Mormon leader named Sam Brannan opened a store in California and started the region's first newspaper. When he heard gold had been found, he opened a mining supply store in Sutter's Fort. He wrote about the gold in his newspaper to attract new customers to his store. Brannan became the first millionaire of the California Gold Rush. He used his money to buy land around San Francisco.

Prospectors look for flakes of gold in a stream in California.

The First Discovery

★ **Chance find sparks gold rush**

★ **Marshall makes nothing**

James Marshall worked as a carpenter. On January 24, 1848, while he was building a new sawmill for John Sutter, Marshall saw something shiny in the river. It was gold. Within a year, thousands of **prospectors** arrived in California to find their fortune. The sawmill was forgotten, and Marshall did not make any money from his discovery of gold! In Canada, the discovery of gold along the Fraser River in British Columbia sparked their first gold rush. Later, the Klondike Gold Rush in the Canada's Yukon made many people rich.

PATH TO THE WEST

★ **Freed slave finds pass**

★ **Tells his life story**

Jim Beckwourth (right) was born into slavery. His mother was a slave and his father was her master. Young Jim was sent to school to be trained as a blacksmith. Becoming a free man in the 1820s, Beckwourth headed west and later joined the California Gold Rush. In 1851, he discovered a pass through the northern Sierra Nevada. Thousands of settlers reached California through Beckwourth Pass. In 1856, Beckwourth told his story in *The Life and Adventures of James P. Beckwourth*.

DID YOU KNOW?

Many prospectors headed for California by ship. They sailed down the East Coast to Panama, crossed through the jungle to the Pacific Coast, then took another ship north to San Francisco.

Getting the Message Through

During the 1800s, increasing settlement and new technology made communications in the West far easier than they had been before.

All Aboard!

★ **Stagecoach routes throughout the West**

★ **Mail and passengers delivered**

Wells, Fargo & Co. delivered goods, mail, and people throughout the West. It also offered banking services to the growing Gold Rush population in California. The Wells Fargo stagecoach lines connected St. Louis to San Francisco. The trip took 25 days or less.

Right: Traveling by stagecoach was uncomfortable—especially for passengers on the outside.

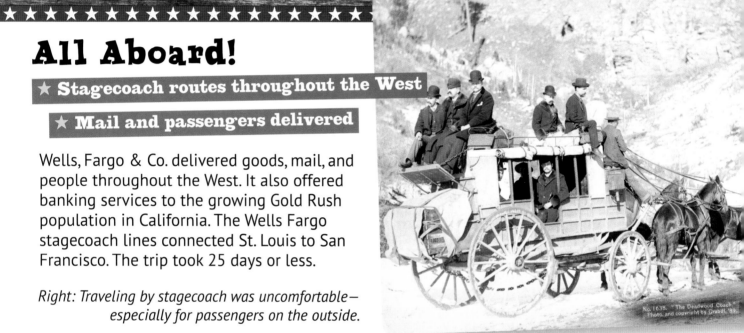

No. 1638. "The Deadwood Coach."
Photo. and copyright by Grabill. '89

DID YOU KNOW?

Although horses were used to pull stagecoaches, heavy loads of supplies were carried in carts pulled by oxen. The oxen were far stronger than horses—but they were also much slower.

Pony Express

★ **Horseback service**

★ **Riders in relay**

In 1860, the Pony Express began as a horseback mail service. Dozens of riders carried deliveries in **relay** from station to station between Missouri and California. Each rider covered up to 75 miles (121 km) a day, and the whole journey took just 10 days. But the Pony Express only lasted two years. It was expensive to run, and it was replaced by the telegraph in 1861.

MR. MORSE'S REMARKABLE INVENTION

★ Telegraph changes the West

★ Instant communication

Samuel Morse, Joseph Henry, and Alfred Vail invented the telegraph in 1836. It used an **electromagnet** to send electrical pulses along a wire. In order to make the telegraph useful, Morse also invented a code to allow people to send messages. Morse Code consisted of short and long pulses. There was a different combination of three pulses for each letter and number.

Right: This engraving shows Samuel Morse and his electric telegraph.

WESTERN UNION

★ Send messages anywhere ...

... but don't use many words

In 1861, the telegraph company Western Union joined with California companies to build the first **transcontinental** telegraph line. Telegraph operators tapped out a sender's message using Morse Code. At the receiving end, another operator translated the message into words and wrote them down. The message was then delivered. Because senders had to pay for each word, messages were very short.

MY WESTERN JOURNAL

Imagine you had to send a telegraph using as few words as possible to save money. How would you tell someone about a day you had at school, for example?

Building the Railroads

The first transcontinental railroad was completed in 1869. Its construction had taken many years of effort by laborers and engineers.

ENGINEERING THE RAILROADS

★ **Crossing the Sierra Nevada**

★ **Frémont finds the way**

Before railroads could be built, engineers and **surveyors** had to identify the easiest route for a train to pass along. In 1853, the explorer and politician John C. Frémont led his fifth expedition to the West. He crossed the Rocky Mountains and Sierra Nevada in winter to prove it was possible to get through the snow. His work was the basis of the route later identified and used by the Central Pacific Railroad.

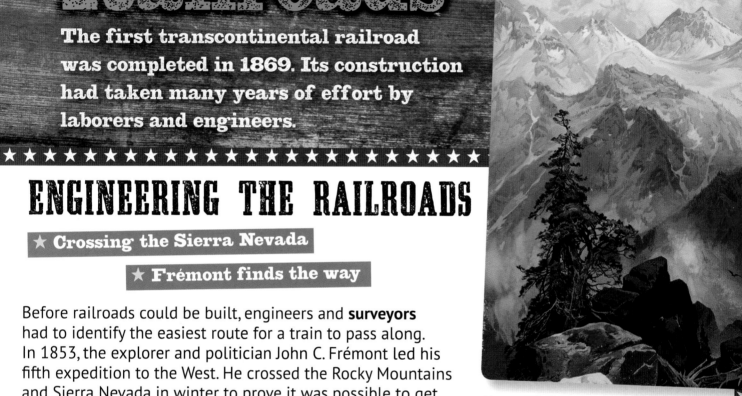

Above: The mountains of the Sierra Nevada were a huge barrier to travelers heading to California.

DID YOU KNOW?

Theodore Judah persuaded four merchants to invest in the Central Pacific Railroad: Collis Huntington, Leland Stanford, Charles Crocker, and Mark Hopkins. They became some of the richest people in the United States. They were known as the "Big Four."

Crazy Judah

★ **Engineer eyes mountains**

★ **Determined to overcome obstacle**

In the 1850s, the engineer Theodore Judah decided to build a railroad through the Sierra Nevada to link California to the rest of the country. The task was so huge, people called him "Crazy Judah." Judah became chief engineer of the Central Pacific Railroad and chose a route through the mountains. Judah's route became part of the transcontinental railroad.

THE TYCOONS

★ **Investors make a fortune ...**

... while laborers lay tracks

The railroads were paid for by private investors, not the government. Some investors lost huge sums of money on railroad schemes that failed, but others made huge fortunes. They included **tycoons** Jason "Jay" Gould, Cornelius Vanderbilt, and Collis P. Huntington. They were called **robber barons**—businessmen who control natural resources and treat workers unfairly. The robber barons came from many different backgrounds. Vanderbilt, for example, had been born poor but worked hard to become one of the richest men in America.

A railroad construction gang at work.

The Empire Builder

★ **Railroads in the north**

★ **Hill runs the show**

James Jerome Hill (left) was a Canadian-born businessman. Born poor, he left school at 14 and worked as a grocer and, later, as a bookkeeping clerk for a steamboat company. He was good at math and eventually bought his own company. In 1873, Hill and some other investors bought the failing St. Paul and Pacific Railway. They turned it into a huge success. Hill then extended the railroad throughout the northern states into the Pacific Northwest. Because of his great influence, Hill became known as "the Empire builder."

Making Money

The West was a land of opportunity for nearly everyone. Some of the earliest successful businesses were set up by immigrants and former slaves.

NEWSPAPER MAN

★ **Publisher writes commandments**

★ **Attracts tourists to California**

James Mason Hutchings was a publisher in California. He printed newspapers for miners and made a fortune when he published his "Miners' Ten Commandments." They were simple rules all miners should follow. In 1855, Hutchings was one of the first visitors to the Yosemite Valley. He promoted the area in his *California Magazine*, making Yosemite popular.

Left: Yosemite became a national park in 1890, after Hutchings helped attract visitors there.

DID YOU KNOW?

Levi Strauss moved to San Francisco in 1853 to expand his family business selling clothes and fabrics. In the 1870s, he teamed up with a tailor named Jacob Davis to make workpants from a strong material called denim. They reinforced the seams with rivets. The men had invented the famous Levi's jeans!

Taming Deadwood

★ **Bullock brings order ...**

... then makes lots of money

In 1876, Seth Bullock moved to Deadwood in the Dakota Territory to open a hardware store with his partner, Sol Star. Deadwood was lawless. The gunfighter "Wild Bill" Hickok was shot dead there the day after Bullock arrived, and the town asked Bullock to become sheriff. Bullock cleaned up Deadwood. It became a safer place to do business. He and Star went on to open a hotel, a ranch, and a flour mill.

African-American Businessman

★ **Ford not allowed to mine**

★ **Makes a fortune from hotels**

Barney Ford and his wife Julia traveled to Colorado during the California Gold Rush. As an escaped slave, Ford was not allowed to **stake** a mining claim. Instead, he opened a barbershop, a restaurant, and several hotels. He became one of the first successful African Americans in the West. By 1870, he was one of the richest men in Colorado. Today, he is often seen as a civil-rights pioneer.

Above: The house Ford had built for his family in Breckenridge, Colorado, is now a museum.

LURE OF THE WEST

★ **Immigrants open stores**

★ **Goods straight from China**

Tens of thousands of Chinese **immigrants** arrived in the western United States and Canada in the 1840s and 1850s to work in mines or on the railroads. Many returned home, but many also stayed. They faced **discrimination** from European settlers and sometimes lived together in "Chinatowns." Some Chinese immigrants opened businesses such as laundries and stores to cater to other Chinese workers. These shops sold goods from China, such as tea, rice, and herbal medicines.

Left: Chinese storekeepers wear their best clothes to celebrate Chinese New Year.

Battles and Displacement

For Native peoples, the arrival of explorers in the West began their struggle against governments attempting to take their land.

ON THE WILD FRONTIER

★ Crockett opposes US expansion

★ Treaties take Native lands

In 1830, President Andrew Jackson proposed the Indian Removal Act. It would force Native peoples to move west of the Mississippi, allowing for settlers to take over their land. Famed **frontiersman** and Congressman Davy Crockett opposed the act and lost his seat in Congress. Similar treaties were passed in Canada. These made sure that Native nations would give up their land to live on reservations, and settlement could continue without Native resistance.

The Indian Removal Act

★ Law forces Native peoples out

★ Jackson ignores protests

The Indian Removal Act allowed President Jackson to force Native Americans to move to "Indian Territory" in the West. The act's supporters said it would preserve the tribes and avoid conflict. Its opponents believed the United States should honor its treaties with Native peoples. They thought settlers and Natives should be able to **coexist** peacefully.

Right: The Cherokee head west on what they called the "Trail of Tears."

The Trail of Tears

★ Fate of the Cherokee

★ Ross fights removal

In 1828, John Ross was elected Chief of the Cherokee nation in Georgia. He was part Cherokee and part Scottish, and grew up in both cultures. Ross opposed the Indian Removal Act, but some Cherokee moved west anyway at the end of 1835. By 1838, the army forced any remaining Cherokee to leave. They were taken to Indian Territory (now Oklahoma) on what came to be called the "Trail of Tears." One quarter of the Cherokee died on the harsh journey.

DID YOU KNOW?

In 1890, a seer or holy man named Wovoka from the Northern Paiute people had a vision. He said that the Native peoples could defeat white settlers taking over the plains by performing a ritual called the Ghost Dance. The dance became popular among Native peoples of the Great Plains.

THE GREAT SIOUX WAR

★ Conflict on the plains

★ Sitting Bull fights back

In the 1870s, a US Army expedition found gold in the Black Hills of the Dakotas. The Black Hills were sacred to the Lakota Sioux. The Lakota leader Sitting Bull convinced several tribes to fight against American settlement of the area. The conflict is known as the Great Sioux War of 1876. Led by Crazy Horse, native warriors won their biggest victory at the Battle of the Little Bighorn on June 25, 1876, killing General George A. Custer and his entire cavalry unit. But that victory alone was not enough. Sitting Bull was forced to make a settlement with the government. The tribes were moved to reservations, opening up the land for white settlement and mining.

Right: Sitting Bull was a spiritual leader of the Lakota Sioux.

Famous Events

Some trailblazers became caught up in major events and movements that shaped the history of the American West.

THE WHITMAN MASSACRE

★ **Oregon mission attacked**

★ **Missionaries slain**

In 1836, a **missionary** and doctor named Marcus Whitman founded a mission in the Willamette Valley of Oregon. He wanted to convert Native peoples to Christianity. In 1847, the local Cayuse people suffered an outbreak of measles. They believed Whitman was to blame. Cayuse warriors attacked the mission, killing Whitman, his wife, and 11 other people.

DID YOU KNOW?

In 1846, a wagon train led by George Donner headed for California. The Donner Party tried to cross the Sierra Nevada in winter. They were trapped by snow for four months. When they ran out of food, they ate human flesh to survive. By the time rescue parties arrived in February, only 48 out of 87 people were still alive.

The Mormon Exodus

★ **Mormons flee intolerance in the East**

★ **Create a settlement in the West**

In 1847, Brigham Young founded a settlement near the Great Salt Lake in what is now Utah. He wanted to found a settlement where his followers would be free to practice their Mormon religion. Over the next 20 years, thousands of Mormons made their way to Salt Lake City along what became known as the Mormon Trail.

Right: Many Americans objected to the Mormon practice of a man having more than one wife, as shown in this family.

The Mountain Meadows Massacre

★ Wagon train attacked

★ Mormon militia blamed

In 1857, a wagon train of families heading to California from Arkansas passed through Utah. Mormon **militia** disguised as Native Americans attacked the wagon train near Mountain Meadows (left). They killed more than 100 of the settlers. Historians believe the **massacre** was caused by the Mormons' fear of outsiders. Mormons were concerned that new American settlers would try to seize their land.

THE EXODUSTERS

★ African American exodus

★ Former slaves settle in Kansas

At the end of the Civil War in 1865, many African Americans wanted to leave the South to escape racism and find better economic opportunities. In 1879, the activist Benjamin Singleton helped thousands of former slaves move to Kansas. The migrants were named Exodusters, after the Exodus in the Bible. The migration continued for years. More than 40,000 former slaves settled in African-American towns in Kansas and elsewhere.

Right: Black settlers leave the South by paddle steamer, heading for Kansas.

Famous Women

The West was dominated by men, but women also played an important role. As successful women in a man's world, they were true trailblazers.

Cashman joined the Klondike Gold Rush in Alaska.

NELLIE CASHMAN

★ **Boarding house owner and nurse ...**

... **joins Alaska Gold Rush**

Nellie Cashman moved west from Boston in 1865. She had ran boardinghouses in mining towns in California and western Canada. Later, she worked as a nurse in Tombstone, Arizona, where she gave much of her money to charity. She went to Yukon and Alaska to prospect for gold during the Klondike Gold Rush of the 1890s.

MY WESTERN JOURNAL

Imagine you were a woman in the West. Using information on these pages, decide what you think would be the best way to earn a living.

Give your reasons.

Doc Susie

★ **Physician in the West**

★ **Town doctor in Colorado**

Born in Indiana in 1870, Susan Anderson moved with her family to Colorado at age 21, where gold had been discovered. She went to medical school in Michigan. After becoming a licensed physician in 1897, she returned to Colorado. She had to work as a nurse rather than as a doctor because she was a woman. She eventually moved to Fraser, Colorado, where she served as the only doctor in town for 49 years. The residents knew her as "Doc Susie."

LUZENA WILSON

★ Woman in the goldfields...
... makes money from home cooking

Luzena Wilson was one of the few women who went with their husbands to the California Gold Rush. During her first six months in Sacramento, she said she saw only two other women. One day, a miner offered her a large sum of money for some of her home cooking—a rare treat in the mining camps. After that, Wilson began a successful career running hotels and restaurants in mining towns.

Biddy Mason

★ Slave wins her freedom
★ Makes fortune in LA

Biddy Mason (right) was a slave who went to court to claim her freedom in 1856. Mason and some other freed slaves headed to California. Mason worked as a nurse and midwife in Los Angeles, which was then a small town. She saved enough money to start buying land, and became wealthy. She gave much of her fortune and time to charity, and became known by the affectionate nickname of "Auntie Mason."

Little Sure Shot

★ Annie gets her gun
★ Ace riflewoman

Around 1875, a teenage girl named Phoebe Ann Mosey beat a circus **sharpshooter** in a shooting competition in Cincinnati. She soon became a star act of Buffalo Bill's Wild West show, performing under the name Annie Oakley. She shot apples off a dog's head and split a playing card through its edge. Sitting Bull, the great Lakota chief, called her "Little Sure Shot."

Right: Annie Oakley learned to hunt as a young girl to support her family.

FAMOUS WOMEN

Famous Outlaws and Lawmen

Some of the most popular stories of the West are about outlaws and the lawmen who chased them. Sometimes there was little difference between the two.

UPHOLDING THE LAW

★ **Earp keeps the peace**

★ **Shootout in Tombstone**

Wyatt Earp was a gambler and gunfighter. As deputy marshal of Tombstone, Arizona, he took part in the gunfight at the O.K. Corral on October 26, 1881. Earp, his brothers, and their friend Doc Holliday faced the Clanton and McLaury brothers in a shootout. Three outlaws died, and Earp's brothers were wounded. Wyatt walked away unharmed.

DID YOU KNOW?

William H. Bonney, or Billy the Kid, is the most famous outlaw of the Wild West. Legend says he killed 21 men, but the total was probably only eight. Billy was captured, but shot his way out of jail. Sheriff Pat Garrett, who was a friend of Billy's, tracked and killed him in 1881.

The Wild Sheriff

★ **Wild Bill keeps the peace ...**

... but shoots his own deputy!

James Butler "Wild Bill" Hickok was a lawman in some of the wildest western towns. In 1865, he killed a gambler in the first "quick-draw" gunfight. In Abilene in 1871, he accidentally shot and killed his own deputy. Hickok won many gunfights, but on August 2, 1876, he was shot in the back while playing cards in Deadwood.

Right: Wild Bill Hickok draws his revolver to keep the peace in Abilene.

THE MOUNTIES

★ **Policing the far northwest**

★ **Gold Rush kept under control**

In Canada, the North-West Mounted Police, or Mounties, were formed in 1873 to keep order in the remote Northwest Territories. Their responsibilities included enforcing treaties with Native peoples and controlling the whiskey trade. In 1897, a small force of Mounties arrived in Yukon to police the Klondike Gold Rush. They enforced the law, taxed prospectors, and made sure everyone heading to the goldfields took enough supplies. The Klondike was one of the most peaceful gold rushes in history. In 1920, the North-West Mounted Police became part of the Royal Canadian Mounted Police.

Above: This Mountie was photographed in the early 20th century. The Mounties had a reputation throughout North America for effective law enforcement.

Bank Robber

★ **Butch steals a fortune**

★ **Heads to South America**

Robert Parker (right) was a Mormon brought up in Utah who later changed his named to Butch Cassidy. After starting his criminal career as a horse thief, Cassidy went on to become the must successful bank and train robber in US history. He led a gang known as the "Wild Bunch." Cassidy was said to never have killed anyone, but the Pinkerton National Detective Agency chased him for years. He escaped to South America with his partner Henry Longabaugh, the "Sundance Kid." The pair were probably killed in a shootout in Bolivia in 1908.

End of the West

In 1890, the US Census Bureau declared that the Frontier was now closed. The trailblazers had helped to open the whole West to settlement. The region was now fully absorbed into the United States.

The Dawes Act

★ **Native land seized**

★ **Poverty grows worse**

By the late 1800s, many Americans believed the best way to live peacefully with Native peoples was to **assimilate** them into American society. In 1887, the Dawes Act began to move Native Americans off their **reservations**. Those who chose to leave were given their own allotment of land and US citizenship. In fact, the program increased poverty among Native Americans. It also allowed the government to claim back large areas of reservation land.

DID YOU KNOW?

One way the United States and Canada tried to assimilate First Nations in the 1890s was by sending children to residential schools. The schools forced children to speak English, changed their names, and made them practice Christianity. Residential schools had a devastating and lasting impact on Native culture, peoples, and communities.

The Gilded Age

★ **Tycoons dominate culture**

★ **Signs of wealth still survive**

The 1870s to the early 1900s was a period known as the Gilded Age. In cities such as New York and San Francisco, the wealthy lived in great luxury. Many families, such as the Astors and Rockefellers, owed their fortunes to businesses in the West, such as fur trading, oil, or railroad construction. They were sometimes criticized for the way they **exploited** the country's natural resources and its people.

Left: Madeleine Astor was married to John Jacob Astor IV. They were among the richest people in New York society.

THE CITY ON THE SALT LAKE

★ **Mormon capital thrives**

★ **Everyone welcomed**

The area of the Great Salt Lake in Utah has a harsh natural environment. Even the Native Americans of the region only lived there during the spring. The Mormons who settled there in 1847 were so eager to find somewhere new to live that they learned to farm the dry land. The city they built is still thriving today. Over half the population of Salt Lake City (left) are non-Mormons. It is one of the fastest-growing cities and most popular places to live in the United States.

THE TOURIST TRAIL

★ **The myth of the West ...**

... reenacted daily

The Wild West was already fascinating readers and theater-goers at the end of the 19th century. Today, people are just as fascinated by tales of the trailblazers. Tourists come from all over the world to visit historic sites and national parks. Visitors can even herd cattle on ranches and attend reenactments of famous gunfights in the places where the original gunfights took place.

Actors reenact the Gunfight at the O.K. Corral in Tombstone, Arizona.

GLOSSARY

ambushed Attacked by someone who is hidden from view

assimilate To absorb someone into another culture

blazed Marked a trail for the first time

coexist To live together at the same time

dime novels Cheap paperback novels that told dramatic and sensational stories

discrimination The unfair treatment of people on the grounds of their race, religion, or other factors

electromagnet A magnet created by passing electricity through a coiled wire

exploited Used a resource in an unfair way

frontier The edge of a settled area

frontiersman Someone who lived in the wilderness

immigrants People who move to a new region or country

interpreter Someone who translates what someone says into another language

manifest destiny The idea that the United States would inevitably claim ownership of the whole of North America

massacre The brutal killing of many people

militia A military force made up of civilians

missionary Someone who tries to introduce their religion to a foreign land

mountain man Someone who lived and worked in the wilderness beyond human settlement

prospectors People who look for useful or valuable minerals

relay A system in which someone performing a task is replaced by another, and so on

reservations Areas of land given to Native American tribes

resources Things that can be put to use, such as minerals, crops, or wood from trees

robber barons Ruthless and unscrupulous businessmen

sharpshooter A person who has excellent aim with a gun

stake To mark the boundaries of a piece of land to claim ownership of it

surveyors People who measure and record land, often for construction purposes

trailblazers People who are the first to do something

transcontinental Describes something such as a route that crosses a whole continent.

treaty An agreement between two groups or nations

tycoons Powerful, wealthy businessmen

wilderness An uninhabited and uncultivated land

April 30: The United States buys the vast Lousiana Territory from France under the Lousiana Purchase.

November 7: An expedition to Oregon led by Meriwether Lewis and William Clark reaches the Pacific Ocean.

March 2: Texas declares independence from Mexico. After a war, Texans create the Republic of Texas in 1836.

December 29: Texas becomes part of the United States.

1803 1804   1808   1835 1836   1838   1845   1847

President Thomas Jefferson sends expeditions to explore the West.

April 8: John Jacob Astor founds the American Fur Company, which employs trappers in the West.

Cherokee living in the East are forced by the US Army to travel to Indian Territory (modern Oklahoma) along the "Trail of Tears."

July 24: The first Mormons found Salt Lake City in Utah Territory, after traveling along the Mormon Trail.

ON THE WEB

www.pbs.org/lewisandclark/
A PBS site about the Lewis and Clark expedition, including an interactive map.

www.history.com/topics/inventions/transcontinental-railroad
A page from History.com about the building of the transcontinental railroad, with links and videos.

www.cherokee.org/AboutTheNation/History/TrailofTears.aspx
A page from the Cherokee Nation with a short history of their forced removal along the "Trail of Tears."

www.pbs.org/opb/historydetectives/feature/women-of-the-wild-west/
A PBS *History Detectives* investigation into the roles women played in the West.

BOOKS

Cook, Diane. *Pathfinders of the American Frontier* (Exploration and Discovery). Mason Crest Publishers, 2002.

Morley, Jacqueline. *You Wouldn't Want to Explore with Lewis and Clark!* Turtleback, 2013.

Perritano, John. *The Transcontinental Railroad* (True Books: Westward Expansion). Scholastic, 2010.

Suen, Anastasia. *Trappers and Mountain Men* (Events in American History). Rourke Publishing, 2006.

January 24: Gold is discovered at Sutter's Mill in California, starting the California Gold Rush.

Western Union erects telegraph lines throughout the West, putting the Pony Express out of business.

May 10: The first transatlantic railroad line is completed at Promontory Point, Utah.

Lakota Native Americans and their allies fight the US Army in the Great Sioux War. They are forced to surrender the following year.

1848 **1861** **1862** **1869** **1876** **1890**

February 2: At the end of the Mexican–American war, California and the Southwest become part of the United States.

May 20: The Homesteader Act makes it easy for settlers to claim up to 160 acres (65 ha) of public land in the West.

The US Census Bureau announces that the Frontier is now closed. All of the United States is now settled.

INDEX

A

African Americans 19, 23, 25
Ashley, William H. 10
assimilation 28
Astor, John Jacob 10

B

Beckwourth, Jim 13
Billy the Kid 26
Black Hills 21
Boone, Daniel 6
Brannan, Sam 12
Bullock, Seth 18
businesses 18–19

C

California 5, 8, 18, 24
California Gold Rush 12–13
Canada 4, 7, 13, 27
Carson, Christopher "Kit" 11
Cashman, Nellie 24
Cassidy, Butch 27
Cherokee peoples 20, 21
Chinatowns 19
Clappe, Louise 25
Clark, William 6, 7
communications 14–15

DEF

Dawes Act 28
Donner Party 22
Exodusters 23
Ford, Barney 19
Frémont, John C. 11, 16
fur trappers 10-11

G

Ghost Dance 21
Great Sioux War 21

H

Hickok, Wild Bill 18, 26
Hill, James Jerome 17
Hudson's Bay Company 10
Hutchings, James Mason 18

IJ

Indian Removal Act 20, 21
Jackson, Andrew 20
Jefferson, Thomas 4, 6
Judah, Theodore 16

KL

Klondike Gold Rush 13, 24, 27
Lewis, Meriwether 6, 7
Little Bighorn, Battle of the 21
Louisiana Purchase 4, 6, 9

M

Mackenzie, Alexander 7
map 8–9
Marshall, James 13
Mason, Biddy 25
Mormons 12, 22, 23, 29
Morse, Samuel 15
mountain men 10–11
My Western Journal 12, 15, 24

N

Native peoples 4, 11, 20–21, 28
North-West Mounted Police 27

O

O.K. Corral 26, 29
Oakley, Annie 25
Oregon 5, 8, 22

P

Pattie, James O. 11
Pike, Zebulon 7
Polk, James K. 5
Pony Express 14

R

railroads 16–17
reservations 28
residential schools 28
"robber barons" 17, 28
Ross, John 21

S

Sacagawea 7
Salt Lake City 22, 29
Sierra Nevada 13, 16, 22
Singleton, Benjamin 23
Sioux peoples 21
Sitting Bull 21, 25
Strauss, Levi 18
Sutter, John A. 12, 13

TU

telegraph 15
Texas 5, 8
Trail of Tears 20, 21
transportation 14–15, 16–17
trappers 10–11
Utah 22, 23, 27, 29

WY

Wells, Fargo & Co 14
Wild West 29
Williams, William S. 11
Wilson, Luzena 25
women 24–25
Wovoka 21
Yosemite Valley 18
Young, Brigham 22
Yukon 13, 24, 27